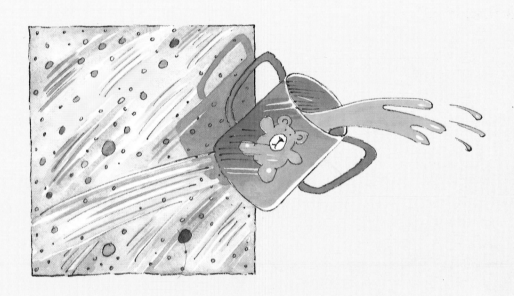

For Poppy, my cat.

THE
HIGHGATE
COLLECTION

Published in New Zealand by
Nelson Price Milburn Ltd
1 Te Puni Street, Petone

This edition published in the United States in 1990 by
Steck-Vaughn Company
P.O. Box 26015
Austin, Texas 78755
Steck-Vaughn Company is a subsidiary
of National Education Corporation.

Bossy Bessie and Solomon Brice
ISBN 0.8114.4272.1
Text © Hope Hucklesby
Illustrations © Nelson Price Milburn Ltd
© 1989 Nelson Price Milburn Ltd

Printed in Hong Kong
by Colorcraft

BOSSY BESSIE AND SOLOMON BRICE

Written by Hope Hucklesby
Illustrated by Philip Webb

A S B

Agapanthus Solomon Brice
Won't eat carrots
And he won't eat rice.
He won't drink coffee
And he won't drink tea.
He won't go swimming
In a salty sea.
He won't grow thin
And he won't grow fat.
He won't do this
And he won't do that.

B B

Bossy Bessie Badminton
Bossed the whole day through —
Wearing silk and satin
And boots of brilliant blue.

Bossy Bessie Badminton
Bossed people young and old —
Wearing a shiny waistcoat
Threaded with silver and gold.

Bossy Bessie Badminton
Bossed Bertram till they wed.
She made him wear pants of purple
And a jacket of pillbox red.

Bossy Bessie Badminton,
She bossed her little son.
She bossed his little sister,
And playmates
. . . *everyone!*

Bossy Bessie Badminton,
She bossed until she died.
"How I *miss* my Bossy Bessie,"
That barmy Bertram cried.

MY SORT OF CAT

He's a 'sit on the shelf -
look after myself'
sort of cat.

He's a 'don't think I care -
I'll sit here and stare'
sort of cat.

He's a 'stroll off alone -
while you're on the phone'
sort of cat.

He's an 'eat what I like -
sardines, cod, or pike'
sort of cat.

A 'proud, sweet, and cozy,
dreadfully nosy'
sort of cat.

He'll never admit it
(probably spit it)
but he loves me
and I love him.

He's *my*
sort of cat.

NO PROMISES

I feel like being *horrible*
and *cross* and VERY *bad* . . .
I feel like driving *everybody*
mad, *mad*, MAD!

I can't *help* being horrible
and nasty, now and then.

I might be right, with any luck,
by half past ten.

PROBABLY NOT

Sarah was jumping as high as the sky
from the bed to the chair to the cot.
Sarah said, "Mummy, can *you* do this?"
Mummy said, "Probably not."

Sarah was turning around and around
getting quite dizzy and hot.
Sarah said, "Mummy, can *you* do this?"
Mummy said, "Probably not."

Sarah was eating some chocolate fish
— in fact she was eating a *lot*!
Sarah said, "Mummy, can *you* eat this much?"
Mummy said, "Probably not."

CLEVER CATS

I love to watch those clever cats
who calmly twist an ear
and look just where they wish to look . . .
yet hear *all* they *want* to hear.

A cat has such a cozy coat.
No need to dress each day.
No need to knit or sew or shop . . .
just stroll outside and play.

A cat can feel completely free
to sleep or eat or play
or find a secret shady spot . . .
(They sometimes hide *all day*!)

What fun to sleep without a sheet,
curled up like a ball!

But what I like to watch the best
is
a cat
climbing down
a wall.

THREE WOOLLY SHEEP

Three woolly sheep!
Three woolly sheep!

See how they run!
See how they run!

They run up the hill
and down again. . . !

They're running
towards the shearing men. . . !

The dogs are guiding them
Into the pen . . .

Into the arms
Of the shearing men. . . !

Three bare sheep!
Three bare sheep!

MY GREEN UMBRELLA SCHOOL

I've got my Mummy's shoes on
And my Daddy's big straw hat.
I've got Grandpa's green umbrella
And my beads from Aunty Pat.

I'm going to sit in Daddy's greenhouse
On his yellow wooden stool
And pretend that I'm a teacher
At the Green Umbrella School.

I'll teach the snowdrops how to curtsy,
Show the sunflowers how to sing,
Then I'll water them all with dewdrops
From a watermelon spring.

I'm going to ring the bluebells
When I sit on Daddy's stool,
And teach the plants their lessons
In my Green Umbrella School.

FEELING SAD

Today I'm feeling rather sad.
I really don't know why.
I've got so much to make me glad —
And yet I want to cry!

SAM'S VISITORS

Some special friends are coming to stay!
They're arriving at half past one!
Let's get ready to greet them all!
We're going to have such fun!

There's an elephant coming from Africa,
Some birds from Timbuktu,
A buffalo from the U.S.A.,
And a monkey from Bombay Zoo.

Australia's sending a koala.
There's a kiwi from New Zealand.
South Africa's sending an ostrich —
Or maybe they'll send an eland.

England has offered a big brown cow,
And Russia a dancing bear.
A frog is coming across from France,
And a tiger from Vanity Fair.

Some special friends are coming today!
They're arriving at half past one!
Sam's meeting them at the train.
It's going to be MARVELOUS fun!

THE SNAKE WHO WANTED A BIKE

Guess what my snake wants?
A *motorbike!*
What a very strange thing
For a snake to like!

How will he reach the handlebars,
The pedals and the seat?
He's got no hands for holding on!
He's got no legs and feet!

14

VERY CLEVER

She can dance
she can sing
she can peep
she can fling
she can hop
she can crawl
she can run
she can fall
she can wink
she can fly
she can blow
she can cry
she can smile
she can write
she can paint
she can bite.
There's a lot
she can do
though she is
only two!

FUNNY GIRL

Candy is a funny girl.
She thinks
the moon is ice,
the sun real gold,
the sea just juice,
and hailstones . . . uncooked rice!